Thank you for hel┄

Jen and Sander

Vinny the Vaquita

Written and illustrated by
Jen Gabler

Story and artistic direction by
Sander Gabler

Illustrations of corals based on photographs by Jackie Mears, http://www.SailMakai.org

First Printing, 2016
ISBN 978-1-943992-00-3
Library of Congress Control Number: 2016903286

www.jengabler.com
Jacera Publishing

Vinny the Vaquita

When nurtured,
the smallest minds
can dream
the biggest dreams.

Vinny the Vaquita was a porpoise with black eyes.
He looked quite like a dolphin, but was a smaller size.
The Gulf of California's where these porpoises are from;

Since Vinny had been born, he'd lived there, following his Mom.
When Vinny the Vaquita was still a baby calf,
He'd giggle, jiggle, wriggle, and he would always laugh.

But all of that had changed, now that Vinny was half grown,
Because he found that, nowadays, he was all alone.
You see, Vinny was the only Vaquita in the Bay,

And so, one day, poor Vinny felt that he must go away.
Vinny hoped that, if he went to some far distant shore,
He'd find that he was not the last and there were still some more.

Just like all Vaquitas, little Vinny was quite shy,
But he'd never know the answer if he didn't try,

So Vinny waved "goodbye" to the place that he called home,
And, for the first time in his life, he began to roam.

Vinny searched both here and there, he looked both high and low;
He went with the current, and he swam against the flow,
But nowhere little Vinny tried even gave a clue,

And soon the little porpoise began to feel quite blue.
He felt his strength was failing with each flap of his tail,
Then he saw an awesome sight: a great, enormous...

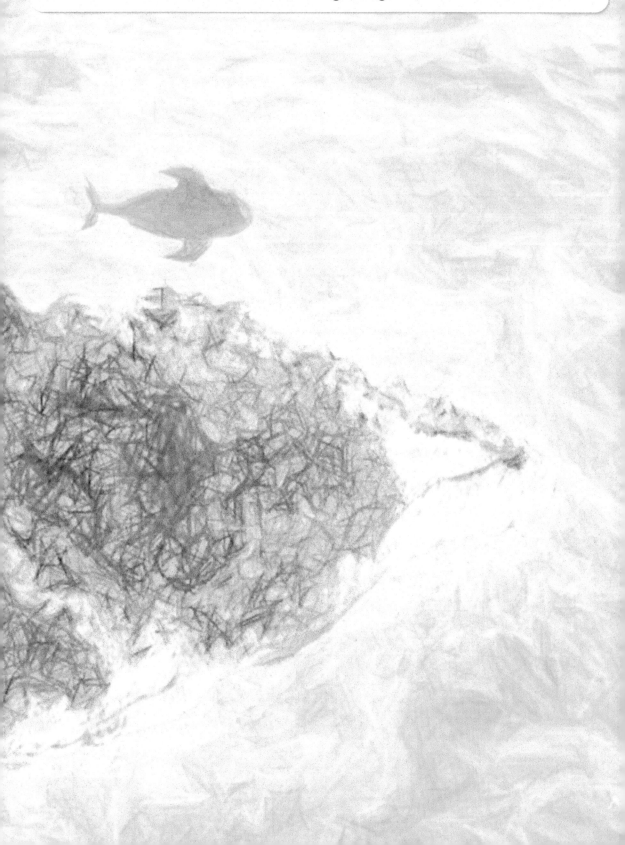

Whale! Vinny tried to find a place that he could go and hide,
But, before he knew it, it was right there by his side.
"Hello! My name is Ronnie," the great big creature said,

And Vinny saw a giant smile on his giant head.
"Sorry you were scared; I didn't mean to cause a fright."
"I'm quite like a Humpback Whale, except I'm called a Right."

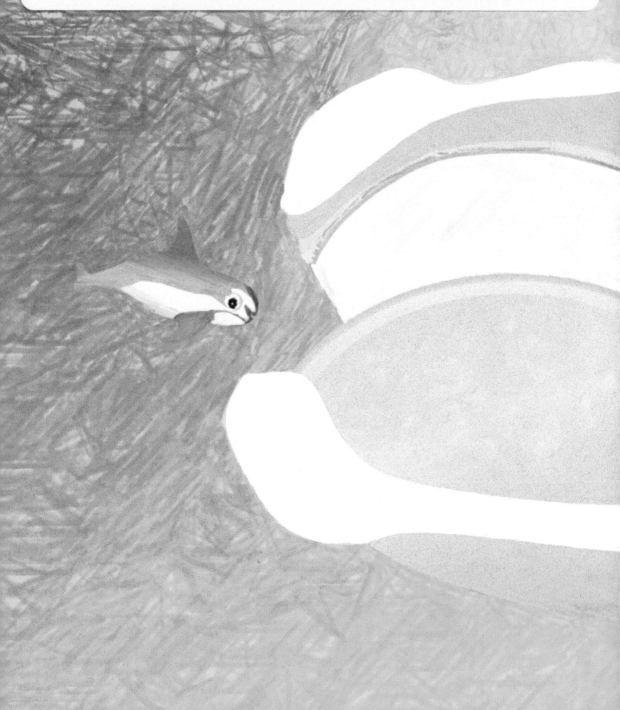

"I couldn't eat a porpoise: I don't have any teeth!"
"Instead, I have baleen on top, and nothing underneath."
"Though I'm one thousand times your weight, you eat bigger food:"

"Squid, shrimp, grunts and sea trout, swallowed whole, not chewed."
"The biggest food that Right Whales eat are teeny, tiny krill,"
"So please don't worry I might bite, as I never will."

Vinny looked at Ronnie, said "It's nice to meet you, sir."
"I should not have jumped, I just did not know what you were."
"I've never seen a Right before, though I see whales each day:"

"Humpbacks, Killers, Fins and Blues, and even, once, a Gray."
"None of them would notice me, I'm smaller than their tails,"
"But I can show you where they are; it's easy to spot whales!"

Ronnie patted Vinny gently with his great big fin,
And cleared his great big throat before he gave a gentle grin.
"You might be small, but there are lots of features that we share:"

"To start, we are both mammals, drinking milk and breathing air,"
"We move our tail flukes up and down, not side to side like fish,"
"And we would play the whole day through, if we could have our wish."

"No, Vinny, it is you I want to talk to, my young lad."
"I couldn't help but notice that you look very sad."

"Would you like to splash and breach? Or play a game of chase?"
"Tell me what to do to put a smile back on your face."

"Thank you, Ronnie, sir. That's really very kind of you,"
"And if you wouldn't mind, there is one thing that you could do."
"I'm sure that you are very loud when you try to be."

"I want to know if there are more Vaquitas than just me."
"Could you ask the other whales if they would look around"
"To see if any others of my species can be found?"

First Ronnie called in Fin Whale and then he called in Gray,
Asking all the whales around to each check in a bay.
Vinny and his friend began to check La Paz inlet,

When a whale called out: "Vaquitas in a fishing net!"
"You really need to get here as quickly as can be;"
"They're all very tangled and I cannot get them free!"

Without a pause for breath, the two new friends started to go,
But when they reached the fishing net, they began to slow.
What they saw was unlike anything they'd seen before:

One hundred whales and dolphins, and maybe even more!
Vinny saw the net holes these cetaceans must have made,
And knew that they'd all come here to try to lend their aid.

Vinny looked to see if the Vaquitas had been saved,
Then Ronnie pointed out where seventeen small creatures waved.
Their eyes were black, like Vinny's, their smiles were just as big,

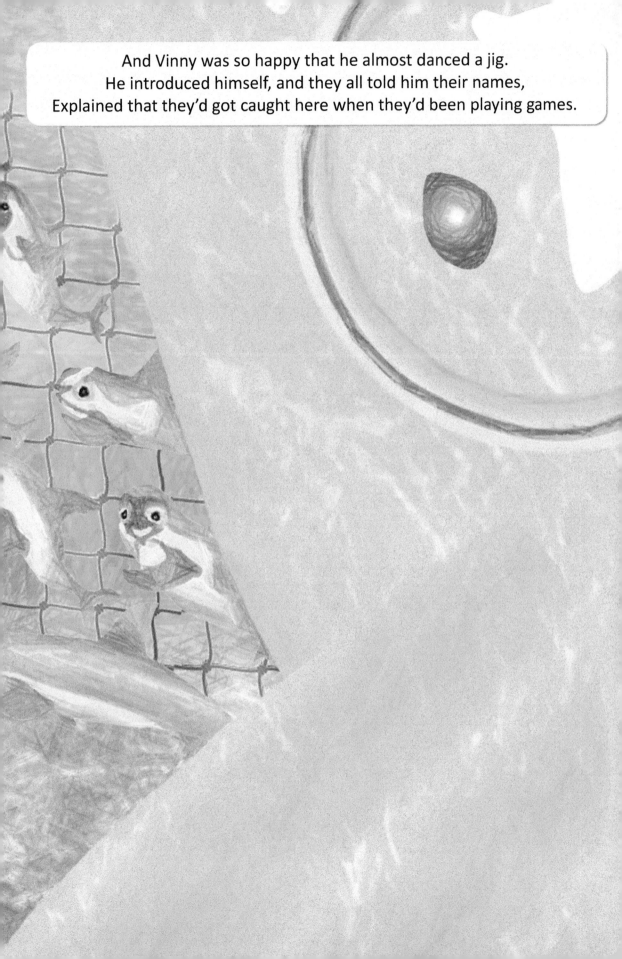

And Vinny was so happy that he almost danced a jig.
He introduced himself, and they all told him their names,
Explained that they'd got caught here when they'd been playing games.

A Killer Whale had found them, and they'd been very scared,
But then the other whales came and they'd realized she cared.
The biggest of Earth's creatures, Sue the Blue Whale, had reversed,

And she had charged the net full speed; her hole had been the first.
Then other whales and dolphins had joined in with a shout,
And, soon, all the Vaquitas had managed to get out.

Now one of the Vaquitas took Vinny by the fin.
"We need to get the word out; will you help us to begin?"
"We need to tell a story, one that nobody forgets."

"We need to tell the fishermen to change to safer nets."
"And, while we're at it, tell the children they can help us, too."
"Cleaning rivers, shores and streets are three things they could do."

Ronnie grinned and nodded, "Let me add to this great plan."
"Ask the children to recycle everything they can,"
"And never let balloons go, they can drift out to the sea,"

"And then they look like jellyfish, and choke whales up, you see."
"If people did these few small things, we wouldn't just survive,"
"Dolphins, whales and porpoises would all begin to thrive!"

Vinny thought a moment, then had a great brain wave.
He found that this adventure had made him very brave.
He flapped his tail with courage and headed to the beach,

And found a little boy there, whom Vinny hoped to teach.
I think you might have heard of him, he's named after the sand.
The boy loved all cetaceans; of course he'd lend a hand!

Vinny is now friends with him, and with his sister, too,
But little Vinny'd love to be special friends with you.
So could you please help Vinny, even in a little way?

Tell grown ups all about him? Tell children when you play?
Tidy up your area, or raise some cash to give?
The world will be far better if we help Vaquitas live!

Glossary

Baleen ('Bay-*leen*'): Instead of teeth, some whales have baleen 'sieves', which let them take in big mouthfuls of water and food and then filter out the water. Baleen plates are made of something like our fingernails.

Blue whale: A blue whale is a baleen whale that is probably the largest animal to have ever lived. They were hunted until they were almost extinct, and there are only a few thousand now alive.

Breach: When a whale jumps out the water, it's called 'breaching'. We don't think vaquitas actually breach.

Cetacean ('Se-*tay*-shun'): Whales (including dolphins and porpoises) are officially called 'cetaceans'. They are mammals, and so need to swim to the surface to breathe, and the babies (called 'calves') drink their mothers' milk.

Dolphin: Oceanic and river dolphins are two families of whales.

Flukes: A whale's tail is made up of two flukes.

Killer whale: Killer whales (or orcas) are very social members of the dolphin family. Like lions, they are top predators. They are intelligent, with very clever ways of hunting. They've even been known to attack and kill sharks, including the great white, as well as other species of whale.

Krill: Krill are small crustaceans (like shrimp and crabs), and are usually only 1/2 to 1 inch long. Krill live in every ocean, and one species alone weighs more than all humans combined.

Porpoise: There are seven species of porpoise alive today, including the vaquita. They are closely related to dolphins, but have shorter beaks and their teeth are a different shape.

Right whale: There are three species of right whale: Southern, North Pacific and North Atlantic. Ronnie is a North Pacific right, (though, in reality, he'd be gray, not green). They are all baleen whales, and have rough patches of white-looking skin ('callosities') on their heads. They are slow and peaceful, and they float when dead, which meant that they were hunted very close to extinction, and all three species are still endangered.

Vaquita ('Va-*kee*-tah'): 'Vaquita' is Spanish for 'little cow'. They're the smallest cetaceans and have dark areas around their lips and eyes. Vaquitas echolocate and communicate with high-pitched calls. They usually swim and rise to the surface slowly, and keep away from people. Vaquitas only live in the Gulf of California, where they are often accidentally trapped in illegal gillnets. In 2014, it was estimated that there were fewer than 100 still alive.

Whale: Whales are marine mammals that are split into two groups: baleen whales and toothed whales. See the next page for more details.

Charities you can donate to:
Research: marinemammalcenter.org/science/Working-with-
               Endangered-Species/vaquita.html
Education: vivavaquita.org
Safer nets: sospecies.org/sos_projects/mammals/vaquitas
Other information and opportunities:
Documentary: wildlensinc.org
Blog and book: vlogvaquita.com
Club: sites.google.com/site/muskwaclub
Adopt a vaquita, petitions, products, and more from the author:
               jengabler.com

Baleen

Right & Gray*

Bowhead

Gray

Pygmy right

N. Atlantic right

N. Pacific right

Southern right

Rorqual

Blue

Bryde's

Common Minke

Eden's

Fin

Humpback

Omura

Sei

Southern Minke

Sperm**

Sperm

Dwarf sperm

Pygmy sperm

Beaked†

Andrew's beaked

Baird's beaked

Blainville's beaked

Cuvier's beaked

Gervais' beaked

Ginkgo-toothed beaked

Gray's beaked

Hector's beaked

Hubbs' beaked

Northern bottlenose

Perrin's beaked

Shepherd's beaked

Sowerby's beaked

Spade-toothed

Tropical bottlenose

Modern day
Cetaceans
From Vinny the Vaquita by Jen and Sander Gabler

*   The Gray whale and Pygmy right whale each form a family of their own.
    They are grouped here for ease of viewing.
** The Dwarf and Pygmy sperm whales form a family of their own.
    They are grouped here for simplicity of viewing.
†   Only a selection of the 21 species in this family are pictured here.
†† Only a selection of the 39 species in this family are pictured here.

Toothed

Narwhal & beluga

Beluga

Narwhal

Oceanic dolphin[††]

Atlantic spotted

Commerson's

Common

Common Bottlenose

Heaviside's

Humpback

Irrawaddy

Right whale

Risso's

Spinner

False killer whale

Killer whale

Melon-headed whale

Pilot whale

Pygmy killer whale

River dolphin

Amazon river

Araguaian river

Baiji (functionally extinct)

La Plata

South Asian river

Porpoise

Burmeister's

Dall's

Finless

Harbour

Spectacled

Vaquita

Yangtze Finless

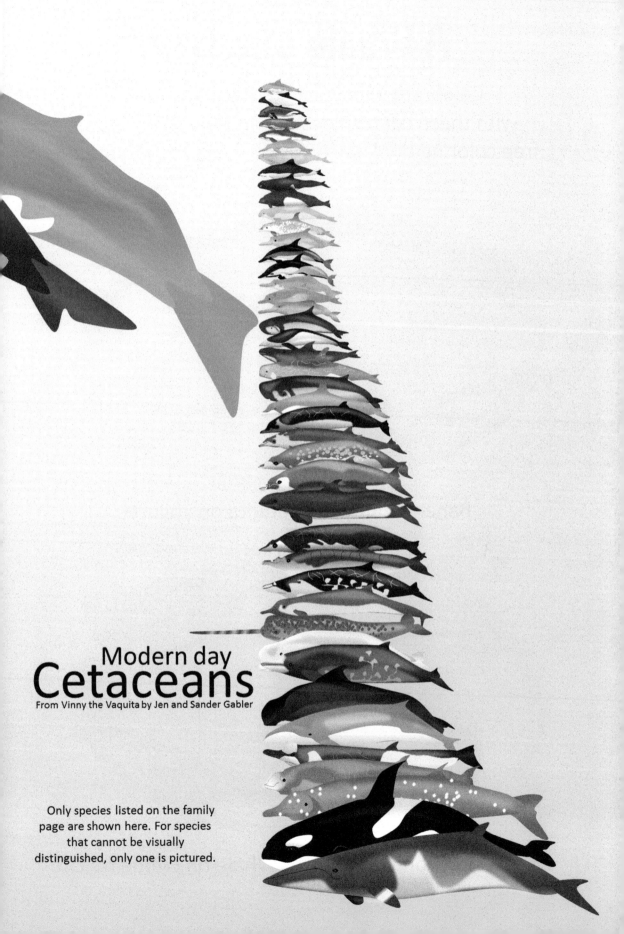

Modern day
Cetaceans
From Vinny the Vaquita by Jen and Sander Gabler

Only species listed on the family
page are shown here. For species
that cannot be visually
distinguished, only one is pictured.

A Whale of a Day!

Celebrate with the cetologist in your life
with these centerpiece and gift ideas, and print
free coloring book party favors from vivavaquita.org

Banana Vinny the Vaquita on yogurt

Cantaloupe Ronnie the Right Whale on crème fraîche

Vinny the Vaquita cake topper in fondant icing

Adopt a vaquita at jengabler.com

CPSIA information can be obtained
at www.ICGtesting.com
Printed in the USA
LVOW06*0524130416

483305LV00007B/12/P